Contents

Written by Lisa Regan
Illustrated by Angelika Scudamore

First published 2015 by Brown Watson
The Old Mill, 76 Fleckney Road
Kibworth Beauchamp
Leicestershire LE8 0HG

ISBN: 978 0 7097 2294 6
© 2015 Brown Watson, England
Reprinted 2016, 2018 (thrice)
Printed in Malaysia

Now I Can
READ
Princess Stories

Brown Watson

ENGLAND

Daisy's Special Day

Today is Princess Daisy's birthday. She is very excited! Later, she is having a party. All of her friends are invited.

Princess Daisy visits the royal kitchen. They are preparing the party food. She has asked for all of her favourite things. The cook is hot and busy. She is making sandwiches and salads, and cakes and pastries. The naughty princess steals a fairy cake. 'I just want to try them!' she laughs.

One of the girls in the kitchen is Princess Daisy's best friend. She is called Katy, and when she isn't working, the two of them play together. They are happiest in the palace garden, playing catch.

Katy is too busy to play right now. She has to help with the cooking and decorating. Then she will be allowed to join the party, and play all of the games.

As the party begins, the guests all arrive. They have brought presents, and Princess Daisy is very excited. Look at all these toys!

Katy looks a little bit sad. She is scared that Princess Daisy won't like her present. But the Princess claps her hands with joy when she opens it. It is her very own daisy chain, and Katy made it herself. Thank you, Katy!

As the party begins, the guests all arrive. They have brought presents, and Princess Daisy is very excited. Look at all these toys!

Katy looks a little bit sad. She is scared that Princess Daisy won't like her present. But the Princess claps her hands with joy when she opens it. It is her very own daisy chain, and Katy made it herself. Thank you, Katy!

Read these words again

party	present
invited	garden
guests	brought
kitchen	allowed
birthday	excited
friends	scared
cooking	favourite

Read these words again

party

invited

guests

kitchen

birthday

friends

cooking

present

garden

brought

allowed

excited

scared

favourite

What can you see here?

balloon

cupcake

tiara

saucepan

present

water fountain

Fun and Games

Sometimes, Princess Elodie loved being a princess. Sometimes she didn't. Like today, when her father had guests for lunch, and she thought it was going to be very boring.

Luckily for Princess Elodie, the President had brought her daughter, and she sat at the lunch table next to Elodie. She was good fun, and they giggled together and ate cake.

After lunch, the two princesses were allowed into the garden to play. Elodie took Soraya's hand and they ran behind the flower bushes. It was very muddy. They were going to get in such trouble!

The girls could see tiny footprints in the mud. Soraya put her finger to her lips, and beckoned for Elodie to follow her. They crept through a tiny hole, deep into the bushes.

A little rabbit sat in front of them, cleaning its paws. 'Well, you took your time!' it said crossly. 'I thought you were never going to find me! Do you want to play, or what?'

The girls gasped, but nodded eagerly. Soon, they were having such fun, chasing the little rabbit around the roots and branches. Before they knew it, it was time for tea – after they'd had a bath, of course!

Read these words again

before   sometimes

rabbit   together

table   through

muddy   branches

bushes   cleaning

garden   trouble

father   daughter

What can you see here?

grapes

butterfly

bird

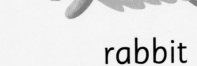

rabbit

apple

flowers

A Magical Place

Have you ever gazed at a rainbow and wondered where it goes to? Princess Charlotte always did, whenever one appeared at her window on a sunny but rainy day.

On one of those days, Charlotte was playing in her room, when she heard a tap-tap-tap on the glass. To her surprise, a tiny little man was outside! 'Follow me!' he said.

Princess Charlotte opened the window and climbed out. The little man took her hand, and together they soared up into the sky, climbing high into the clouds.

The rainbow was amazing. It smelt of all of Charlotte's favourite things: milkshake and grass and her mother's perfume. Every step they took made a twinkling sound, and released little sparks of colour everywhere.

As they reached the top of the rainbow, Charlotte gasped. It was a fairground land, with music and balloons and lots of other princesses whirling around on the rides. What fun!

All too soon, the little man took Charlotte's hand and said they had to go. The rain had stopped, and the rainbow would disappear. But now Charlotte can't wait for those special sunny, rainy days!

Read these words again

sunny	colour
sparks	outside
follow	special
window	perfume
sound	climbed
clouds	soared
surprise	disappear

What can you see here?

rainbow

tent

big wheel

purse

teddy

helter skelter

29

Practice Makes Perfect

Princess Lily was cross. She was learning new ballet steps, and she couldn't get them right. 'Oh, how I wish I had a fairy godmother, or some magic dancing shoes!' she grumbled.

But, do you know what? She didn't. Even though she wished and wished, no fairy appeared to wave her magic wand. Her boring ballet shoes stayed in the corner where she had thrown them.

At her next ballet lesson, Miss Sylvie asked Princess Lily if she had been practising. 'No,' she admitted, grumpily. 'The steps are too hard.'

Miss Sylvie carefully explained the steps again. Then she waved her baton in the air and counted in time to the music. 'Just follow me!' she said to Lily.

Back at home, Lily unpacked her bag and was going to throw her shoes in the corner again. Instead, she put them on, and began to practise the steps she had learned. Gradually, they got easier and easier.

As Lily concentrated, and remembered what Miss Sylvie had shown her, her shoes grew lighter on her feet, and the steps flowed without her trying. Perhaps Miss Sylvie was a fairy godmother, after all!

Read these words again

music   right

trying   easier

follow   gradually

dancing   instead

wished   perhaps

baton   ballet

counted   lighter

What can you see here?

lamp

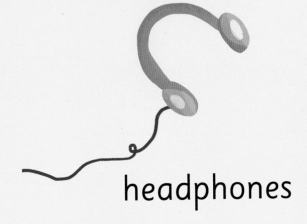

headphones

goldfish

ballet shoes

cushion

cat

All Change

Princess Gloriana was excited. It was the day of the grand royal ball, and she had a whole new outfit to wear. She tried it on and admired herself in the mirror. It was stunning!

As the guests arrived, Gloriana looked out of the window. Oh! One of them was wearing the same tiara. That would never do! She quickly changed hers, and ran downstairs.

Halfway down the staircase, she spotted another princess wearing the same gloves as hers. No way! She ran back upstairs and put on a different pair.

As she crossed the hallway, she saw a very important guest wearing the exact same shoes as she had chosen. Grr! She quickly ran back and grabbed another pair from her royal wardrobe.

Poor Gloriana! The next
princess she saw was wearing
an identical necklace, and another
one had on matching earrings. She
became very cross indeed. She did
not want to wear the same as
ANYONE else. She wanted to
look special!

Finally, Princess Gloriana entered
the ballroom. Her mother took one
look at her and gasped. 'Why,
Gloriana! How, erm, special your
outfit is! You will surely be the
belle of the ball!'

Read these words again

outfit

indeed

mirror

gloves

wearing

changed

finally

another

different

wardrobe

downstairs

admired

matching

quickly

What can you see here?

crown

portrait

shoes

gloves

mirror

necklace

45

A Secret Princess

Once upon a time, there was a girl called Bethany, who was very unhappy. She lived with her wicked stepmother, who spent all the family's money on her own daughters.

There was no money left for Bethany, so she had no shoes, and clothes that were too small. She was left alone all day long, and her only friends were the mice under her bed.

One day, Bethany was so sad that she decided to run away. She crept out of her room and fled to the dark forest. When she could run no further, she sat on a fallen tree and began to cry.

To her surprise, every tear that fell turned into a diamond when it touched the ground! A magnificent stag walked towards her. 'You must be a princess,' he explained.

Bethany did not know what to think. Then the stag asked if she would do him a very kind favour. 'If you cry your diamond tears onto my back, it will break the magic spell.'

When the tears touched the stag, he was transformed into a handsome prince. He invited Bethany back to his palace, and she had all the shoes and clothes that a princess could wish for!

Read these words again

magic

alone

family

wicked

fallen

money

clothes

further

unhappy

diamond

towards

favour

handsome

friends

What can you see here?

chandelier

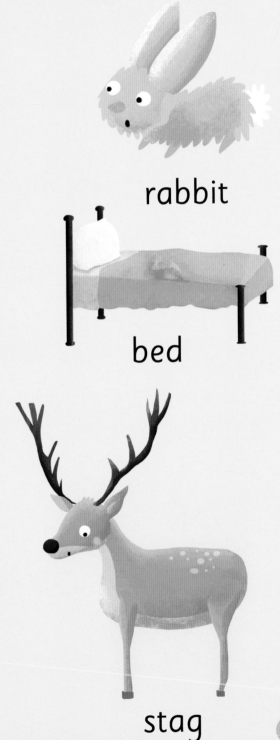

rabbit

bed

mouse

shrub

stag

Fit for a King

Today is King Anthony's birthday. His little girl, Amelia, has baked him a cake. Cook has helped her, of course. It is a large, gooey chocolate cake on a special platter.

Amelia isn't happy with the cake. 'It doesn't look very fancy,' she explains. 'It is supposed to be fit for a king!' Cook promises she will show Amelia how to make it look extra special.

Cook takes some scissors and paper out of a drawer and hands them to the princess. She tells her to cut out a heart shape. Amelia looks puzzled.

Then Cook puts the paper heart on top of the cake. 'But that's rubbish!' Amelia wails. 'It looks even worse than it did before!' Cook tells her to be patient.

'Now for the finishing touches!' says Cook. She takes a can from the cupboard and shakes it really hard. Then she sprays a golden shimmer over the whole cake. 'Wow!' says Amelia.

But it isn't finished yet. Cook lifts off the paper heart to leave a perfect shape underneath. Then they add lots of chocolate buttons around the edge. 'Made with love, and fit for any king!' they agree.

Read these words again

rubbish

worse

chocolate

underneath

finished

touches

cupboard

shakes

shimmer

patient

extra

supposed

helped

baked

What can you see here?

dog

jars

wooden spoon

plates

cake

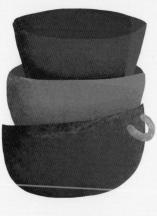

pots

Seeing the Sea

Princess Eleanor lives in a faraway land, full of forests and fields and magnificent cities. She loves it very much. But she has never seen the sea.

One day, her father makes an announcement. 'We must travel abroad,' he says, 'to visit the King of Mersea. It is a watery place, with oceans all around.' Eleanor is very excited.

The royal family travel for many days. The King of Mersea greets them, and takes them to the beach. Princess Eleanor loves it! She splashes around in the waves, and builds a sand castle that looks like her own home.

Then she notices something. 'The sea is running away!' she cries. 'Daddy, make it come back!' Her father smiles sadly. 'Not even a king can command the sea,' he says.

Princess Eleanor is very upset. She sits quietly all evening, and doesn't want to eat or dance at the Royal Ball. She goes to bed early, and cries herself to sleep.

The next day, her father takes her hand. 'Come back to the beach,' he says gently. 'I have something to show you.' And of course, the sea was there again! That made Princess Eleanor very happy indeed.

Read these words again

visit   watery

travel   oceans

waves   excited

castle   command

dance   indeed

early   herself

abroad   notices

What can you see here?

carriage

crab

bucket

palm tree

spade

fish

castle

69

A Secret Staircase

Princess Josephine was bored. She decided to explore the castle. She wasn't sure if she was allowed to wander anywhere she liked, so she tiptoed quietly around, opening all the doors very quietly.

One door looked very different from all the others. It was tiny, with an ornate metal lock and a big key with a jewel on it. Josephine turned it, and crept inside.

The door led to a tiny, spiral staircase, that climbed up and up and up. She must be inside a very tall tower! Josephine hitched up her skirts and huffed and puffed to the top.

As she stood on the final stair, she noticed a window. It was colourful and bright, with a picture of a knight in shining armour. She leant closer to look.

To the princess's surprise, the window glowed, and the knight spoke to her. 'Give me your hand,' he said. As Josephine reached out to touch the glass, there was a flash of light.

She found herself sitting behind the knight and galloping through the countryside. It was astonishing! Now she knows that whenever she is bored, she can join her dashing knight and have lots of fun!

Read these words again

jewel	behind
bored	closer
metal	inside
picture	knight
window	anywhere
explore	quietly
sitting	different

What can you see here?

wall curtain

staircase

candle

deer

flowers

door

The Perfect Princess

There was once a princess called Penelope, who was a very tidy little girl. Her hair was always neatly plaited, and her clothes were always clean. She put away her toys when she finished playing, and washed her hands before every meal.

Princess Penelope's mummy was very proud of her. She was a very tidy queen, and loved her daughter's neatness.

One day, the queen sat on Penelope's bed, and held her daughter's hand. 'I have some news for you,' she said. 'I am going to have another baby!'

Penelope was shocked. How would that work? She had seen babies before, and they were messy, smelly things, with dirty nappies and mushy food on their face. Yuck! She didn't want one in her life.

Princess Penelope went into an enormous sulk. She wouldn't talk to her mummy, even when her tummy grew big and she wanted Penelope to cuddle it.

Then the fateful day came. The queen went into hospital to have her baby. The whole country rejoiced – except for Penelope. Until she went to visit her new sister. 'Oh!' she cried, as she held her sister's tiny hand. 'She's just perfect!'

Read these words again

mummy

cuddle

sister

clean

washed

queen

another

smelly

country

neatly

hospital

enormous

plaited

finished

What can you see here?

picture

books

teddy bear

rug

brush

toy box

Gone Missing

What pet would you have, if you could choose any creature you like? Princess Bianca was such a lucky girl that she owned a unicorn. Yes, her very own unicorn called Verity, to play with whenever she wanted!

The two of them often ran through the palace gardens, and laughed and jumped together. Then Bianca would sit on the unicorn's back, and brush her beautiful mane.

Princess Bianca often wished they could leave the palace, and play in the forest. But Verity refused. 'You can never go in the forest,' she said. 'Your parents would be very cross.'

One day, when Bianca had finished her lessons, she went out to find Verity. But the unicorn was nowhere to be seen. Bianca searched everywhere, but had to go to bed without finding her.

The next day, the Princess
wondered if she should search
in the forest. But she had been
warned never to go there. What
should she do? She was a good
girl, and never broke the rules.

As she sat in the garden,
pondering what to do, she heard
the sound of hooves. She looked
up, and was delighted to see
Verity – with a unicorn foal!
Now she had two wonderful
pets to play with!

Read these words again

rules

foal

lucky

brush

warned

lessons

choose

search

forest

delighted

wonderful

refused

should

laughed

What can you see here?

bee

bird

butterfly

unicorn

tree

beehive